Black Bear Cub at Sweet Berry Trail

SMITHSONIAN'S BACKYARD

For the red-headed cutie, Kaelin Mae Campbell. With love—L.G.G.

For Elaine and all her loving cubs.—W.N.

Book copyright © 2008 Palm Publishing, LLC and the Smithsonian Institution, Washington, DC 20560.

Published by Soundprints, an imprint of Palm Publishing, LLC, Norwalk, Connecticut.
www.soundprints.com

Book design: Shields & Partners, Westport, CT
Book layout: Katie Sears
Editor: Tracee Williams
Editorial assistance: Lisa Odierno
Production editor: Brian E. Giblin
Production coordinator: Chris Dobias

First Edition 2008
10 9 8 7 6 5 4 3 2
Printed in China

Acknowledgments:
   Our very special thanks to Dr. Don E. Wilson of the Department of Systematic Biology at the Smithsonian Institution's National Museum of Natural History for his curatorial review.
   Soundprints would also like to thank Ellen Nanney at the Smithsonian Institution's Office of Product Development and Licensing for her help in the creation of this book.

Library of Congress Cataloging-in-Publication Data

Galvin, Laura Gates.

   Black bear cub at Sweet Berry Trail / by Laura Gates Galvin ; illustrated by Will Nelson.—1st ed.
      p. cm.—(Smithsonian's backyard collection)
   Summary: Follows Mama, Bear Cub, and Brother from early morning until late afternoon as they search for food, cool off in a lake, find honey in the woods, play and explore, and take a nap in a tree. Includes facts about the American Black Bear and a glossary.
   ISBN 978-1-59249-773-7 (hardcover)—ISBN 978-1-59249-774-4 (pbk.)—ISBN 978-1-59249-775-1 (micro book)
   1. Black bear—Juvenile fiction. [1. Black bear—Fiction. 2. Bears—Fiction. 3. Animals—Infancy—Fiction. 4. Forests and forestry—Fiction.] I. Nelson, Will, ill. II. Title.
      PZ10.3.G153Blc 2008
      [E]—dc22
                              2008016495

Black Bear Cub at Sweet Berry Trail

by Laura Gates Galvin

Illustrated by Will Nelson

Soundprints
Where Children Discover...

In the earliest part of the morning when all is quiet, the sun peeks over the horizon. *Chirp, chirp, chirp.* The silence of dawn is broken by a chorus of baby birds. Tiny sparrows sit in their nests with beaks wide open, waiting for breakfast.

Three animals trudge through the forest that borders an old white house on Sweet Berry Trail. One of the animals is very large. The other two, who are following close behind, are much smaller.

It is a black bear and her two cubs. They woke up before the sunrise after a long night's sleep and now they are foraging in the forest for something to eat. Their keen sense of smell tells them that there are berry bushes nearby. They like to eat berries as well as other fruits and plants they can find in the forest.

One of the youngsters, Bear Cub, follows Mama as she lumbers toward the bush. Bear Cub notices red and pink dots covering the bush and sniffs them. The dots are sweet juicy raspberries. The bears have found their breakfast.

Mama and her cubs spend the next hour carefully plucking each and every berry from the bush. Because they don't have fingers, they use their lips to pick off the tasty fruit. Bear Cub eats as many berries as she can find.

A chipmunk hides in a bush nearby waiting for the bears to move on before scurrying out to look for his own meal.

The sun is now shifting higher in the sky and the August morning is growing warm and humid. With a full belly, Bear Cub follows her Mama and Brother through the forest toward the lake behind the old white house. A swim in the lake is just what the bears need to stay cool.

Splash! Mama jumps into the water. *Splash, splash!*
Bear Cub and Brother follow. They are all good swimmers.
While Mama swims across the lake, Bear Cub and Brother
splash and play at the water's edge.

In the distance, a door slams shut. Mama hears the
noise and instantly swims back to the cubs.

Humph, humph. Bear Cub hears Mama making a blowing sound and watches her carefully in case there is danger nearby. Mama stands on her hind legs to see what caused the loud noise. Even though it is quite far from the lake, Mama can see a man standing near the porch of the old white house. Mama is afraid of humans and she doesn't want any trouble for her cubs. She needs to hide her family!

Huma, huma, huma. Mama makes a huffing sound to the cubs, telling them to follow as she bolts out of the water and races through the forest. Bear Cub and Brother stay close behind. For such large animals, the bears can run very fast!

The smaller forest creatures rush to get out of the way as the bears hurry toward a large tree.

As quick as a squirrel, Mama climbs up a tall oak tree. Bear Cub and Brother scurry up behind her. They sit quietly in the high branches for a long time until Mama feels it is safe to come down.

Finally Bear Cub turns to follow Mama down the tree, but wait...what is that buzzing noise? The sound is coming from one of the tree branches.

Mama and the cubs stop climbing. They all listen
carefully. Bear Cub follows the sound with her eyes.
It's a beehive on a nearby branch—what a treat!

Using her sharp claws,
Mama rips open the hive. Hundreds of
little bees swarm from within. Luckily, the bears'
thick fur and tough skin help them from being
stung by the honey bees.

Bear Cub reaches into the nest with her paw
and brings a mound of bees, larvae and dripping
honey to her mouth. She sits in the branches
eating her delicious snack.

After all of the honey is gone, Mama leads the way down the tall oak tree. Bear Cub and Brother follow her to a patch of old damp leaves behind a fallen tree. It is time for a nap. Mama curls up and closes her eyes.

The cubs are not ready to rest so they wander over to a small clearing near the fallen tree.

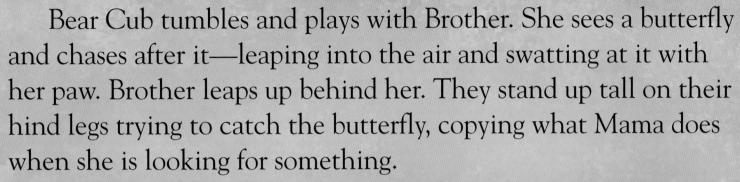

Bear Cub tumbles and plays with Brother. She sees a butterfly and chases after it—leaping into the air and swatting at it with her paw. Brother leaps up behind her. They stand up tall on their hind legs trying to catch the butterfly, copying what Mama does when she is looking for something.

Suddenly, Mama opens one eye and lets out a moan. She is telling the cubs that it is time to sleep. It will be evening soon and they will need energy to look for food again before darkness falls.

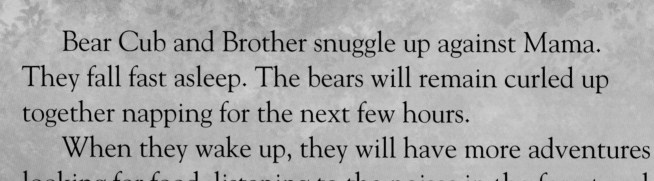

Bear Cub and Brother snuggle up against Mama. They fall fast asleep. The bears will remain curled up together napping for the next few hours.

When they wake up, they will have more adventures looking for food, listening to the noises in the forest and staying away from any people who might be near the old white house on Sweet Berry Trail.

About the American Black Bear

The American black bear can be found in most of the forested regions of the United States and Canada. Black bears are not always pure black in color. In western regions of North America, blonde, cinnamon and honey-colored black bears have been found. The size of black bears varies widely depending on their region, diet and the availability of food. Male bears can be up to 60 percent bigger than female bears, with a length of over 6 feet and weighing up to 650 pounds! On average, female bears rarely reach over 6 feet and weigh more than 175 pounds. Black bears can live up to 30 years.

Even though many people believe that black bears are ferocious animals, they are actually shy and gentle. They rarely attack people and will usually run and hide from humans. Black bears can run up to 30 miles per hour and are great climbers. They will climb trees or stand tall or paw at the ground to defend themselves. They are also heard making a blowing sound when they feel threatened. Black bears do not growl.

In regions with cold winter weather where food becomes scarce, black bears hibernate. In the fall they eat and build up fat layers and then rest for up to seven months. In warmer regions such as Florida, black bears might not hibernate at all. In the spring, summer and early fall, black bears spend the day looking for food and taking frequent naps. If a black bear lives in or near an area that is heavily populated by humans, it will become active only at night to avoid any human contact.

Black bears have a very keen sense of smell and sharp color vision. They also have good night vision due to a reflector system in their eyes that brightens objects in the dark.

Black bears are carnivores, or meat eaters, but a good part of their diet consists of fruit, nuts, berries, plants, insect larvae and grasses. A smaller portion of their diet consists of honey, small mammals, birds and reptiles.

Glossary

cubs: baby bears.

forage: search widely for food or provisions.

huffing: a sound made by letting out a short burst of air.

larvae: the immature form of a bee.

lumber: move in an awkward, heavy way.

scurry: move hurriedly with short quick steps.

sparrow: a small songbird that is found throughout most of North America.

swarm: move in or form a large or dense group.

trudge: slow walk, lifting feet as little as possible.

Points of Interest in this Book

pp. 4-5: chipping sparrows.
pp. 6-7: gold-ringed dragonfly, raspberry canes.
pp. 10-11: eastern chipmunk.
pp. 12-13: great blue heron, dandelions.
pp. 14-15: white-tailed deer, mallard duck.

pp. 18-19: red squirrel, cotton-tailed rabbit, oak tree.
pp. 22-23: honey bees.
pp. 24-25: great horned owl.
pp. 28-29: monarch butterfly.
pp. 30-31: field cricket.